THE SCHOOL IN
MURKY WOOD

THE SCHOOL IN
MURKY WOOD
Malcolm Bird

Chronicle Books
San Francisco

For
Annice Crossley

CIP Data availiable.
ISBN 0-8118-0544-1

Chronicle Books
275 Fifth Street, San Francisco, California 94103

Printed in Singapore.

Text and illustrations copyright © 1992 by Malcolm Bird.
Typography design by Laura Jane Coats.

First published in the United States in 1993 by Chronicle Books.
First published in Great Britain in 1992 by Orchard Books,
96 Leonard Street, London EC2A 4RH

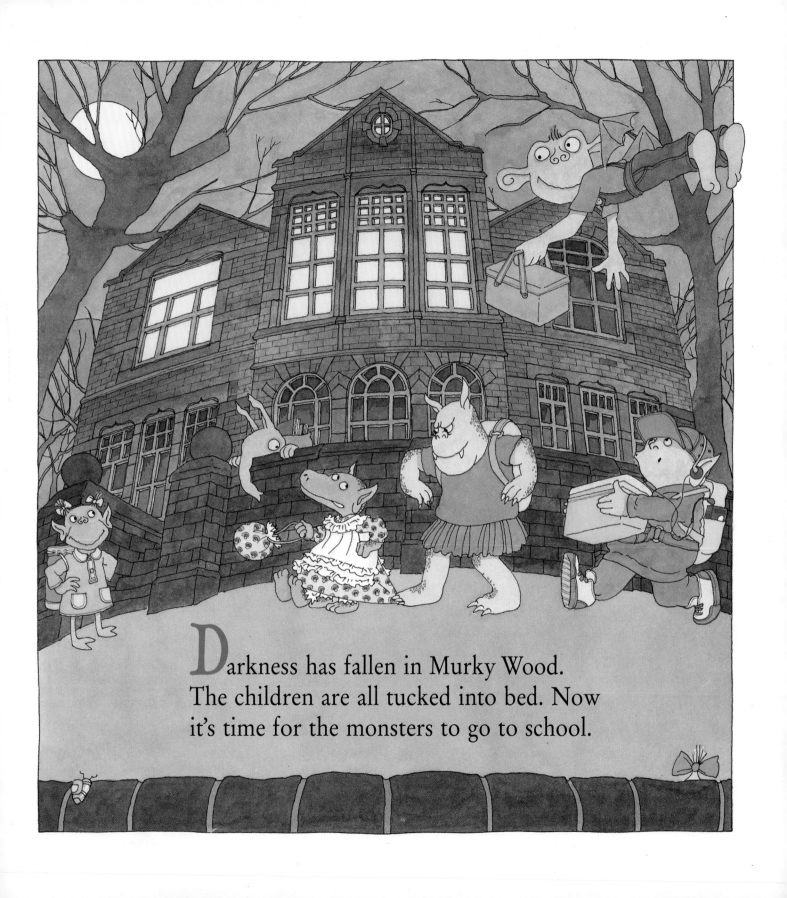

Darkness has fallen in Murky Wood.
The children are all tucked into bed. Now
it's time for the monsters to go to school.

Miss Moist, the teacher, takes attendance by
calling out the names of the monsters in her class.
Tonight everyone is present.

Before lessons begin, the students must look after the classroom pets. Grisly shakes the bats awake while Dampsy and Clammy fetch their favorite snack — flies.

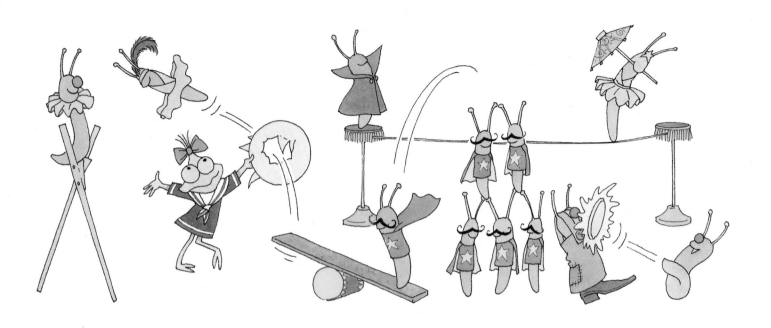

Squirmy teaches the slugs some new tricks,
while Pesky and Grunter let the spiders out
for some exercise.

Then, it's time for the lessons. The monsters in Miss Moist's class are excellent students. Daydreaming, counting the minutes until class ends, and making faces are their favorite activities. And they are the best in the school at not paying attention.

Next the students practice making a mess.

They drop litter on the floor, help the spiders build their webs, separate socks, and put grimy rings around the sinks.

After that, Miss Moist and her class try out a new science experiment. Tonight they are making slime, a delicious monster treat.

Then Miss Moist rings her bell
to announce it's time for dinner.
"Food at last!" shouts her class.

The monsters make a dash for the cafeteria. They love the food that Mrs. Wormold, the dinner lady, has made. It smells really disgusting.

Mr. Brine, the headmaster, is a stickler for bad manners. Snarlene is the best. She has a gold star for chewing with her mouth open.

After dinner, it's time for howling practice —
the best lesson of all. Mr. Brine urges the students
to be as noisy as they can.

The whole building shakes and shudders.
The monsters have never howled so loud before.
Miss Moist is very proud of her class.

In art class Miss Moist poses gracefully
while the monsters express themselves.

They're all very artistic.

Next the monsters settle down to do their own
special projects — like making spooky puppets
or knitting a spaghetti scarf...

or building a robot to frighten their friends.

The last lesson is grumpy dancing. Miss Moist does a demonstration. She stamps her feet and wiggles her toes, waves her arms and wrinkles her nose.

One, two, one, two — the monsters all join in:
stamping, frowning, scowling, snarling,
with grumpy faces for good grumpy dancing!

Before they know it, the sun is rising in Murky Wood. It's time for the monsters to go home. All their things must be taken down and hidden.

Miss Moist checks that the classroom is exactly as they found it, and the monsters start to leave.

Have you noticed anything strange in *your* class lately?